Poor Tuggerisms

Written & Illustrated by Jolie Bell

Book 2 of the Poor Tugger Series

A Book of Canine
Comments, Quips,
Thoughts, Tips, &
Other Fun Stuff
About Dogs

the Peppertree Press

Sarasota, Florida

ISBN: 0-9778525-4-7
Printed in the U.S.A.
Printed August, 2006

To _____

From _____

Date

_____

About Poor Tugger

For Years, the Bell family was willingly subservient to the whims and antics of their Miniature Schnauzer, Tugger, who ranked high on the list of VIP's (Very Impish Pets).

He ruled the roost with an iron will and a soft spot for anyone who would give him a pat or a treat.

In the first book of the series, *Poor Tugger's Almanac of Canine Wisdoms*, Tugger was the *prince of proverbs*. He shared his wisdoms to entertain and to enlighten and allowed readers to see the world from the ground up.

In this book, Tugger's "isms" take you again to a world where dogs have evolved to first-class citizenship. They will leave you with a deeper appreciation for our finest, four-footed, furry friends.

Find out what the world might be like today had dogs scored a bit higher on the evolutionary exam.

Dedication

This one's for all the dog lovers of the world.

It's for Franny with love from Granny.

It's for Steve who takes the business of business seriously and helps me stay organized.

It's for Erynn who makes me happy.

I exist; therefore, I am.
I am special; therefore, I exist in style.

Born free? Not me!
My very impressive pedigree is worth a very impressive fee.

I will gladly pay you Tuesday for a *Lamb-Burger* today.

I think it was Will Rogers' dog that said,
"I never met a man I didn't lick."

You ain't nothin' but a Hound dog,
but I'm a very much renowned dog.

One claw, two claw,
I've got a dewclaw.
Three claw, four claw,
It's on my forepaw.
No, I don't need a medic.
It's not a flaw,
Just something genetic
I got from Ma and Pa.

I've always had a burning ambition
To enter the Westminster competition.
It would make my life complete,
But alas, a mongrel can't compete.

Puttin' on the dog
Milady doth adore,
But people stare agog
When she goes out to the store.

How do you like the split flea soup?
I made it myself from scratch.

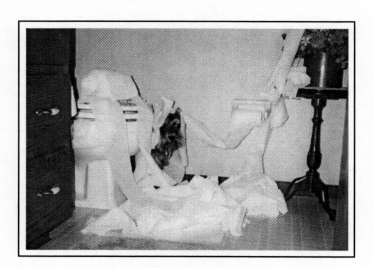

Show me a roll of toilet paper
and I'll show you a very mischievous caper.

A house without a pooch
is like a hug without a smooch...
okay, but not nearly
as nice as it could be.

Lean meat to the left. Lean meat to the right.
Stand up, sit down, bite bite bite!

Every afternoon
Around the hour of four,
A strange phenomenon
Occurs at my front door.
I hear suspicious tapping
I simply can't ignore,
Then suddenly it's happening.
Things are shot through a slot
And tumble to the floor.

I don't appreciate this intrusion.
It causes me confusion.
With a huff and puff
I pounce on the stuff,
Rip and shred
Until it's dead,
Then nestle down to rest my head
Upon the soft and fluffy bed.

There's a dog up in the sky
You can see as dark is nigh.
It's got a star named Sirius.
It watches over us.
Hey, I'm serious!

If you need advice about caring for a puppy,
you could read a book by the famous Dogter Spock.

What's all this nonsense about a Bulldog in a china shop?

In case you didn't know,
Here's an interesting note.
Before I enter a show,
I always strip my coat.

They call this the 'Year of the Reader', or is it 'Breeder'?
Oh well, either way, I'm ready!

A day without a mutt is like a day you're in a rut.

If you follow in my footsteps, wear shoes!

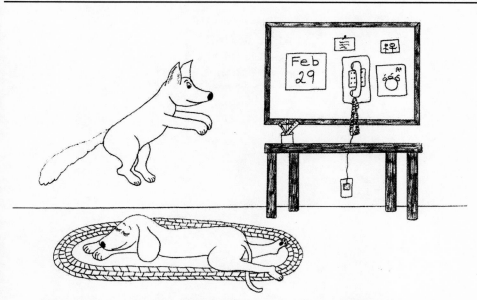

Have you ever wondered why the quick brown fox jumped
over the lazy dog? I have, and I think it was
probably because it was February 29th and he was
playing a game of *Leap Dog.*

Something old,
Something new,
Something borrowed,
Something blue.
Doesn't matter,
I still chew.

Don't be a fool. Stay in obedience school.

Ask not what you can do for your master,
but rather, what can your master do for you
to make your life comfy and cozy too.

Tolling a duck
Takes pluck.
It's a hunting skill
That brings 'em in for the kill.
As part of the sport,
I caper and cavort,
Creating an uproar
To lure the duck ashore.
Such a display
A duck cannot ignore.

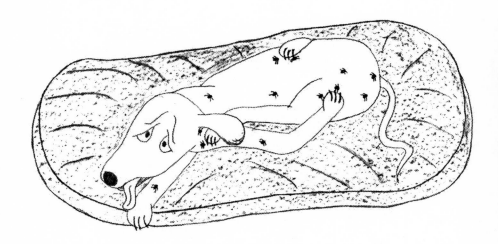

An infested dog is like that famous watch;
it takes a ticking and keeps on licking.

April showers bring May flowers
That I shall plant for hours and hours.
Although it makes my body sore,
They'll be lovely evermore!

Remember Dr. Pavlov?
Several of you may.
Well, what was he a doctor of?
I really couldn't say.

Humans celebrate him
And often over-rate him.
I mean, don't you think it strange
That he never even heard of mange?

He never cured our rabies
Or delivered doggie babies.
He didn't heal our hot spots
Or give us any stinging shots.

He didn't crop our ears
Or check around our rears.
He didn't mend our paws
Or cram pills down our craws.

He didn't treat our worms
Or disinfect our germs.
He doesn't sound like a doctor, does he?
So, what the heck was he?

Something else puzzles me too
And makes me feel like a fool.
How come when I think of him
I always start to drool?

To dare me
Doesn't much scare me,
But if I'm double-dog dared,
Then I may need repaired.

Cats have 9 lives. Too bad they don't have K-9 lives.

Anything you can chew, I can chew better.
I can chew anything better than you.

Dis temper of mine is like a disease!

Don't let the cat out of the bag...just yet.

Okay, last time,
this is your stain...

and this is your
stain on rugs.

A bone of contention
is a stupid invention.
You can't even chew it!

A dog fight can happen anywhere; on the ground or even in the air.

A penny for your thoughts about shots. Will I like them lots?

Physician, heal thyself and stay away from myself.

Ah, home sweet home with my bone sweet bone.

The best offense is de fence!

The sign said *Wet Paint* and I'm a very obedient little guy.

A dog in heat
is a dog I gotta meet.

When I'm at the end of my rope
And can't reach my favorite tree,
I never give up hope,
And, like a dope,
I struggle to get myself free.

I gag and choke
And darn near croak.
My tongue is all droopy and dried,
Then just as I reach my precious oak,
Master takes me inside.

1 for the master.
2 for the show dog.
3 to make a pedigree.
4 to win some dough, dog.

Old dogs don't have the scents they were born with.

Something's Rottenweiler in Denmark.

I'm a little wet behind the ears.
No problem, here's my dryer thingy.

Sitting and staying
Is too much like obeying.
I'd rather be outside
Running about and playing.

If I must say so,
Heiress Total, Soccer-Tease
And Playdoh,
Were three wise sages
Of the early ages,
But when I hear their philosophy,
I admit it's all just Greek to me!

It ain't over 'till the fat lady eats the last bite.

The Armed Forces and me
wear dog tags for ID
to prove we're who we say we be.

De-liver
De litter
Of de canine critter,
De sooner de bitter.
Judging by size
Better advertise
For a qualified puppy sitter.

The only thing I have to fear is the newspaper on my rear.

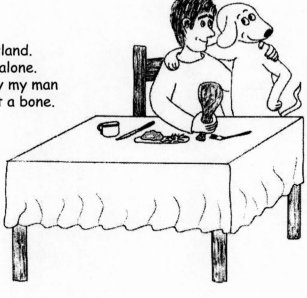

No man is an island.
No man stands alone.
I'll always stand by my man
As long as he's got a bone.

Hocus pocus! Thumpity thump!
If you please,
Make these fleas
Disappear from my rumpity rump.

There's a dogleg in the road
So I've recently learned,
And I'm about to explode
Because no one seems concerned.

I just want to cry
For that poor, little guy,
And I intend to search for him
To offer the aid of an artificial limb.

Don't worry, be yappy!

Phew! It's been a long day and I'm all *Tuggered* out.

The next time it rains while the sun is shining,
I'm going to try to find the legendary
Spot of Gold at the end of the rainbow.

When you've got a pedigree
you've got to be careful not to breed between the lines.

Stand by your man
when he opens your supper can.

So many trees;
so little leash.

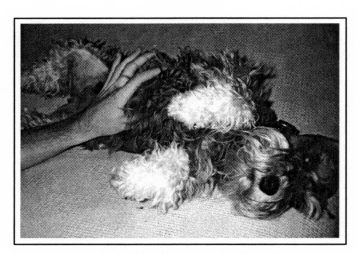

Hey bub! How about a belly rub?
More, more, more I do implore.
And by the way,
Could you keep this up all day?

Mirror, mirror on the wall,
who's the furriest of us all?

Mine eyes have seen the glory of the coming of my meal.

If everyone lit just one little candle,
Such a bright world this could be.
It would also make it easier
To get a good look at cute, little me.

I think I remember an old fable about a dog who had a bone. He looked in the water and saw what he thought was another dog like himself with a bigger bone than his. He couldn't swim, so he tried to grab the other dog's bone but lost his own bone instead. What a disgrace to the canine race, but then it's only a story that's supposed to teach a lesson.

Obviously, the moral of this story is that it's really important for us dogs to learn how to swim so that this kind of thing won't happen. I mean, if that dog had learned to swim when he was a pup, he might have been able to catch that other dog in the water. Then he wouldn't have lost his own bone and he would have had the other bone too.

Hey, I'm pretty good at figuring out stories, aren't I?

It's time I got a new leash on life.

Furry tails can come true.
It can happen to you
if you've got the right brew.

My dog is last but not leashed.

Mark my words, not my territory!

Some Hounds are born with
a silver coon in their mouths.

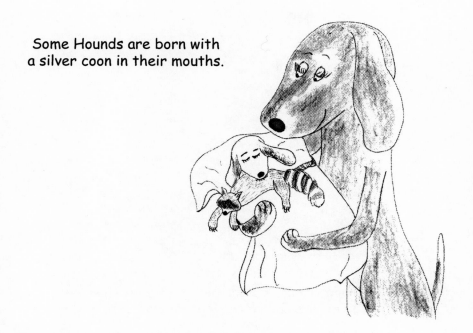

Seldom is heard a discouraging word from my trainer.

To beg or not to beg; that is the question.
Too much begging can lead to indigestion.

If the postman always rings twice,
then he'll simply have to pay the price.

I'd like to be sitting in the lap of luxury.
Actually, sitting in any lap is a luxury.

The gingham dog and the calico cat
Got into a little spat.
Each had a burning passion
To wear a brand new fashion.

They put on stripes
Of all colors and types
And tried on lots
Of polka dots.

Neither agreed,
And so indeed,
They uttered with only a whine,
"Guess we'll just have to resign
To wear the same old-fashioned design."

I think it's ever so much fun taking mistress for her daily run!

One hand washes the other.
Both hands wash me.
I wish they'd wash my brother
So I could wiggle free.

I need all sorts of information for my fancy-schmancy registration:

What's the texture of my fur?
Am I a cur or is my bloodline pure?
Is my build massive or slight?
What's my shoulder height? Am I gentle or do I bite?
Was my sire a gent? If so, for how much did he rent?
Do I have a pleasant temperament?
My coat has how many hues? What kind of flea shampoo do I use?
Have I paid my AKC dues?
What was my dam's maiden name? Was she a champion dame?
Have other relatives achieved any fame?
Have I learned to heel? What do I eat for my evening meal?
How soft do my ears feel?
How much do I drool? What was my rank in obedience school?
Have there ever been worms in my stool?
What is my stance? Do I saunter or prance?
Do I roll over, beg or dance?
Was I raised in a crate?
How many females did I mate? And did I ever procreate?
How often do I snip my claws? Do I have pendulous jaws?
Are there any noticeable flaws?
In what kind of family was I reared?
Does food get lodged in my beard? Am I normal or am I weird?
How long does my tail grow? Will I sell for lots of dough?
These are things I just don't know.

What a bunch of gobbledygook
just to get my name in a special book!

These doggoned little bugs that
burrow under my skin really tick me off.

The good news...
I went to obedience school.

The bad news...
gotta go again!

These adorable Spaniel puppies
warm the Cockers of my heart.

If you go on a chewing spree
And leave a pile of torn debris,
You could stay and sweat it out
And listen to your master shout.
As for me, I simply flee
And hope my master doesn't see.

Today is the first day of the rest of my cushy life.

Though I make myself sick
When I constantly lick,
It's an act I simply adore.
First a slurp, then a burp
Followed by phlegm on the floor.

I've gotta confess
It's compulsiveness;
An urge I can't ignore.
I lick nonstop until I drop
Then lick a little more.

You can take the words out of my mouth,
just don't take the food!

A Dachshund has no trouble making ends meet.

I finally figured out
How to solve the puzzle
Of how to swallow a guzzle
With this wicked muzzle
Fastened to my snout.

Fee Fi Fo Fum.
I smell the Bloodhound of an Englishman.
Be he alive or be he dead,
I'll chew his bones if I'm not fed.

See this flap
Under my chin?
It's called a dewlap.
It hangs where my throat's always been.

Among other things
It dangles and swings,
And often I just want to curse,
But sometimes it's dandy
And comes in quite handy
When I haven't carried my purse.

Ho Ho Ho,
It's Christmas time you know,
But rather than settling down
For a nap in my comfy bed,
I have to be putting up
With this holiday fun instead.

Dog-eared pages
Send me into rages.
It's awfully hard on my head,
So please use a bookmark instead.

One thing that really rubs me the wrong way
is a person who won't rub me at all.

I'm always chasing rainbows.
It's safer than chasing cars I suppose.

Even after the
dog days of summer,
I still feel the heat.

Sock it to me! Sock it to me! Sock it to me!

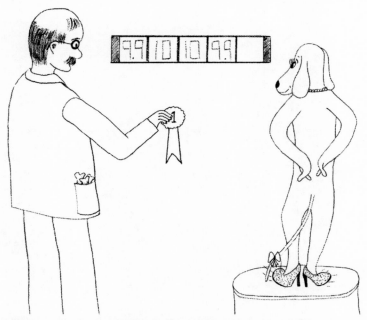

Show dogs, click your heels together three times and repeat,
"There's no place like first place. There's no place like first place..."

If it ever really does rain cats and dogs,
watch out for those puddles, man!

Oh, what a tangled web we weave
while helping Granny knit a sleeve.

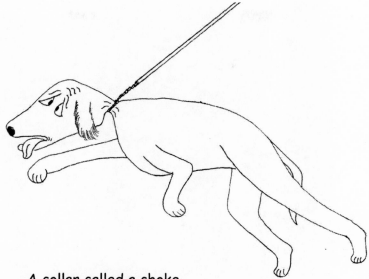

A collar called a choke
isn't much fun for a poor, old bloke.

I just love this tree. It's good to the last drop.

You may not really care,
But guess what?
Most every kind of mutt
Has three different types of hair
From its head down to its butt.
It sounds inane;
So let me explain.

Coarse *guard* hairs form
To keep us dry.
Fine hairs keep us warm
When wintertime draws nigh.
Whiskers are *tactile* hair,
But they don't grow just anywhere.
The only place is on the face.
They're sensitive organs of touch,
And we like them very much.

When I can't keep my cool, I really get hot under the collar.

It'll be a cold day in June
Before I hunt another coon.
My master's given up on me
Cause I keep barking up the wrong tree.

Way too cool for words!

I know a dog named Spot
Who does exactly what he ought.
He's nothing but a wimp.

I never do what I've been taught
Whether I'm punished or not.
Guess I'm nothing but an imp.

When my tummy rumbles,
I don't care how the cookie crumbles.

I'm footloose and fancy free
and I don't have a Cairn the world.

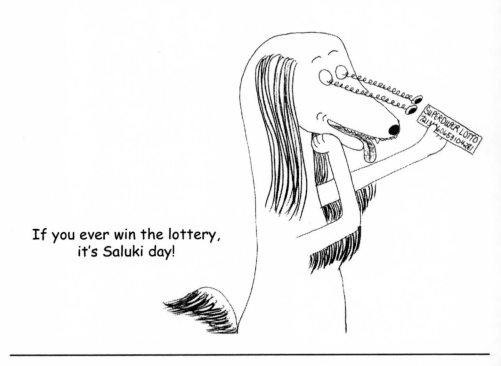

If you ever win the lottery,
it's Saluki day!

Nothin' says lovin'
Like some turkey from the oven.
The people eat the breast.
I get the rest,
But here's a special note,
Don't eat the bone,
For statistics have shown
It could get stuck in your throat.

If you're wanting a tasty meal,
try sinking your teeth into a tender Achilles' heel.

A dog's life isn't always what it's cracked up to be.
I mean, sometimes the pillows aren't even fluffy.

Bye-bye, have a bone voyage!

I'm a stray so much to my sorrow,
I'm here today and gone tomorrow.

I must be a very special dog because wherever I go to visit, people always roll up the red carpet for me.

Just a crazy thought - remember the song that goes "There was a farmer had a dog and Bingo was his name?" Well, was Bingo the farmer or the dog?

When the wind is in the east, the shedding is the least.
When the wind is in the west, the drooling is the best.

Next time you're at the grocery store shopping,
pick up a carton of that new non-dairy topping.

What if I had a clone?
I'd never have to be alone,
But would I have to share my bone?
And would myself still be my own?

I'd always have a friend to play,
But is it okay to duplicate my DNA?
Admittedly, it would be great
To have a facsimile mate.
On the other hand,
Is it really right to mess with fate?

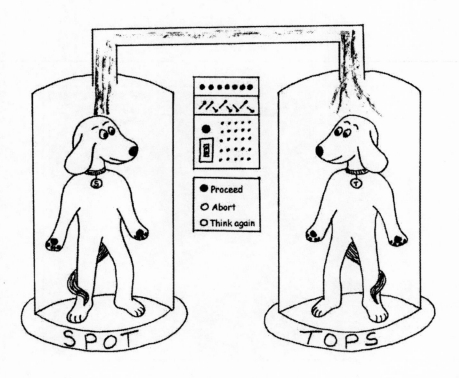

Thou shalt not commit to a dull tree.

I'm dog-tired and need to get wired.

God spelled backward is *Dog*.
I think that makes me kind of special.

Too bad the vet's not in. I'll try to hide my grin.
I have a hunch he's out to lunch.
Guess I'll have to go away and come again another day.

If two roads diverged in the woods,
it would be scents-less if I
should take the one less traveled by.

What do I do whenever I have a new litter?
I Sealy'em with a kiss.

Though mama may be sore,
there's always room for one more.

A stray dog's life is all about
garbage in and *garbage out*.

Don't beat around the bush.
You never know who you'll meet around the bush.

A shave and a haircut - 2 bits,
Except for me.
I have to pay a higher fee
Because of my tangled pits.

I can hardly wait to see my master.
My tail's beginning to wag much faster.
I sure did miss her.
Oh boy, I can't wait to kiss her.

I'm going to lick her pretty face,
But first I'll lick my behinder place.

Don't fence me in.
There are too many places that I've never been.

Faster than a speeding Greyhound,
More powerful than a loco Mastiff,
Able to leap tall fences in a single bound;
Look, up in the sky...
Is it a Bird Dog?
Is it a plain Mongrel?
No, it's Super Mutt!

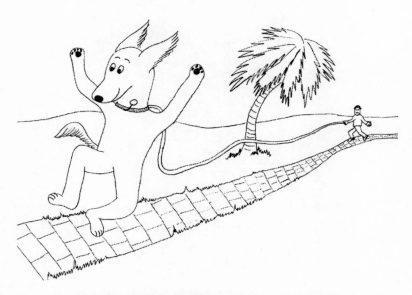

Give me liberty or at least give me a long leash.

I've seen men who were too big for their britches,
and I've seen sires who were too big for their bitches.

I like Dr. B. He's very nice to me.
As far as I can tell, he's the one who keeps me well.

If a tree falls in the woods and no one is there,
Does it make a sound? As if I really care!
The only thing of interest to me
Is that now I'm free to go and pee
On every branch of the beautiful tree.
Yippee!

Yes, we have no bananas.
We have no bananas today,
For Tugger is like the piranhas,
He gobbles them where they lay.

Easy come. Easy go. Easy win for *Best of Show*.

Wake up
and smell the Collie!

An eye for an eye.
A tooth for a tooth.
Canines who fight
Are very uncouth.
Dogs ought to try
To teach their youth
To lick, not bite,
And that's the truth.

Here's something to make you think.
I've always been assumin'
That there's a genetic link
Between a dog and a human.

Nothing but insane?
Balderdash you say?
Well, I believe it's truth,
Otherwise, how do you explain
What's in your mouth today
That's called a *canine* tooth?

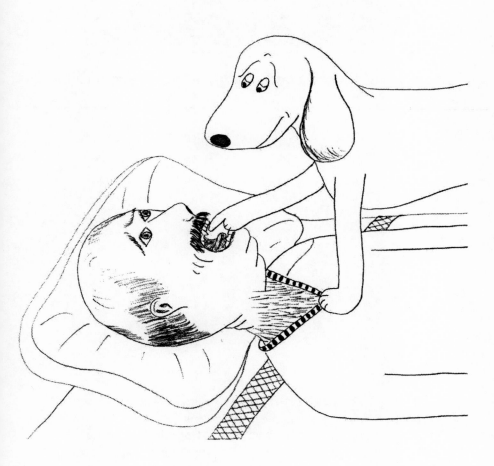

I don't really need a bed, just a place to prop my head.

They say dogs are faithful companions. This is so true.
In fact, I heard that some old geezer out in Yellowstone
Park even built a monument to his dog and he named it
Old Faithful. It's become a famous tourist attraction
because, like the dog, it squirts about once every hour.

I just had a huge litter of Cockerpoos,
so I'll make you an offer you can't refuse.

In fourteen hundred and ninety two
Columbus trailed a Kerry Blue.
Across the world the two of them flew.
Alas, the dog had the sense to stop at the ledge,
Columbus was dense; he fell off the edge!

Yeesh--bad hair day!

The long days of summer
Are really a bummer.
It gets so hot I pant a lot,
So I spend every day hidden away
In a cool and shady spot.

I have a bone to pick with you,
so come on over and have a chew.

When the going gets tough and you've had enough,
it ain't no sin to holler for kin.

I like to stay close on the heels
of the source of my daily meals.

This place has gone to the dogs.

I have a ken I got from my kin.
It's a sense so intense that helps me
When I don't know where I've been.
If I've run astray and lost my way,
It helps me get home agin.

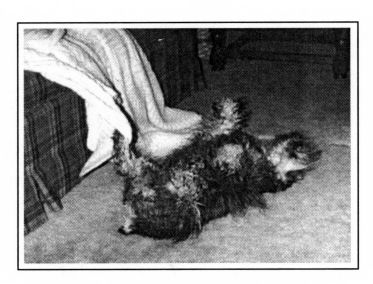

Let the good times roll over!

If you bury the hatchet instead of the bone,
you're likely to catch it when master gets home.

Trying to catch the master's ball really drives me up a wall.

When they put that rope on me, I'm just fit to be tied!

When you're in over your head and things are looking grim,
you've got to make a choice - it's either synch or swim.

Of all the canines that I've polled,
their charge card of choice is the Viszla Gold.

You look as smug as a bug on a Pug.

Here boy!
Come!
Fetch!

Someday my Prince will come,
But for now when I call
Or toss him a ball,
He only stares and acts dumb.

I think I'm getting a double Chin.

Bow wow wow.
I'm in the Army now.
I'll learn to fight
For justice and right
And dine on the finest chow.

Tugger, Tugger, ring your bell.
It's a trick you do so well.
When you want to go outdoors,
Ring the bell, for it is yours.

Ring it when you want to be
In the yard to sniff a tree.
Ring it when you want to play.
Ring it any time of day.

From the day you were born,
Whether night, noon or morn,
Woe is me because, you see,
It is ringing constantly.

Gotta have a little drink, but I can't reach the kitchen sink.
Bottoms up!

Say, who's the jolly good fellow who left this river of yellow?

I'm trying to teach my friend to swim,
But look at him!
It's been an uphill battle
Just to teach him a simple dog paddle.

I think that I shall never see
a restroom lovely as a tree.

What's mine is mine,
and what's yours is mine,
especially when it's time to dine.

I wonder if you realize
That the tapetum lucidum in my eyes
Makes them glow in the dark
Like a neon spark.
They reflect the light
So I can see better at night.

I can often smell the cat,
But if I bell the cat,
I'll always know
Just where she's at.
Then I can get 'er
All the better.

One of the things I like about cats...
They've got retractable claws.
Unfortunately, mine will not do that.
It's one of my very few flaws.

There once was a dog in a manger,
Then something happened to change 'er.
On Christmas Eve night
She saw the star's light
And gave up her bed to a stranger.

Hey look! It's a studbook,
And there's my name.
I think I'll soon have fortune and fame.

So now that I'm one of the greats,
From here on out, without a doubt,
I'll have no problem getting dates.

Being behind the eight ball
Isn't so bad at all.
It's really quite a great ball
To bounce against the wall.

If I could just get my foot in the door,
I might not be *in the doghouse* anymore.

I understand there's a dogfish in the sea.
It's like a shark,
Though doesn't bark.
I doubt it can swim any better than me.

Something wondrous
Once lived under us.
A dog named Cerberus was known,
To have guarded the gates of the underworld zone.

On its shoulders there were
Three unruly heads of fur.
It must have been a silly sight
When all three heads got in a fight.

ET, phone the ASPCA!

This is a special tree
That's named for you and me,
And I feel good,
As any dog would.

There's another type of blossom
That's awesome,
And like the dogwood tree,
It's name refers to me.

The plant life of the hour
Is the dog tooth violet flower,
Although really
It's considered a lily.

Anyway, the canine connection
Is in the design perfection,
For each petal resembles my incisor.
There now, you're all the wiser.

Shore's nice having a slice of paradise.

I don't want to be a drag
Or an old party pooper,
So I take along a pick up bag
Or my super duper scooper.

The guys are always telling me
That makin' whoopee is fun,
But I can't find a recipe
So, I guess I don't get none.

Oops, so sorry. I'm afraid that was my faux paw.

I need a place to call my own
Where I can go to be alone.
When the kids are noisy or causing a riot,
My hideout is comfy and dark and quiet.

A poem by my master:

How do I love my dog?
Let me count the ways.
I love him when he runs and plays.
I love him when he flops and lays.
I love him when he howls and bays.
I love him when he sits and stays
And even when he disobeys.

I love him oh so many ways.
I give him lots of love and praise.
He gets me through my lonely days.
He sets my heart ablaze...
That's how I love my dog!

Sign 'em, Sealy'em and deliver 'em.

It's generally understood
That if you knock on wood
Nothing bad will happen to you
The whole day through.
I firmly believe this is true.

Humans can have a dogma, but they can't have mine!

Oh fudge,
I'm back in Canine Court,
And here comes the judge
With a hefty crime report.

I don't dare budge
But I wish I was free.
Maybe she won't hold a grudge
If I enter an insanity plea.

Occasionally, me and the fox
Go out together for daily walks.
We plan a route
For our walkabout,
Determine home base,
Establish a pace
Then cut right to the chase.

Today's run:

1. Start with a trot from this very spot.
2. Proceed to Blueberry Hill then to the old grist mill.
3. Left 500 feet to the end of Mulberry Street.
4. Around the corner past the home of Dr. Warner.
5. Then assuming you're still able, go all the way to the horse's stable.
6. Reverse it all for the final leg. Last one home is a rotten egg.

When you're out to dine
And your appetite is small,
A doggie bag is fine,
But wouldn't it be better
To take along your Setter
And just let 'er finish it all?

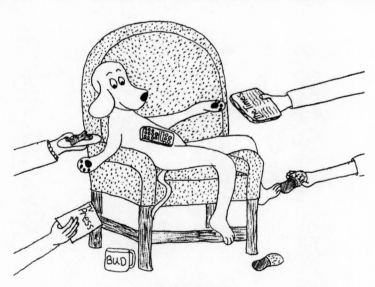

Only fools
Play by house rules.
I play by my own
And basically rule my family's home.

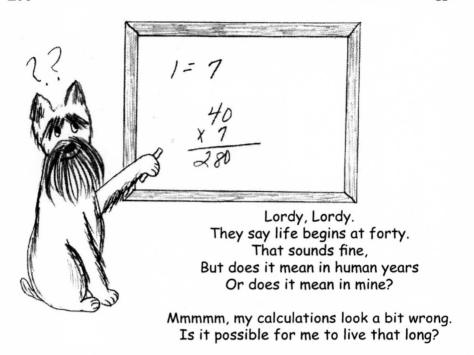

Lordy, Lordy.
They say life begins at forty.
That sounds fine,
But does it mean in human years
Or does it mean in mine?

Mmmmm, my calculations look a bit wrong.
Is it possible for me to live that long?

Sorry señor, no can obey. No hablo inglés today.

Doggone it is an expression.
Say it with aggression
Or use it with discretion;
Either way, it makes an impression.

I have a yen
For a Japanese Spitz.
On a scale of 10,
Right above 20 she sits.

When her female aura emits
The essence of estrogen,
I'm driven outta my wits,
Causing a shortage of oxygen
That sends me into a frenzied blitz.

Something special I can do
Is hear a high frequency pitch
The likes of which
Cannot be heard by you.

I don't mean to be terse,
But there's nothing worse
Than constantly hearing
Doggerel verse.
I say poo poo to it
And would certainly never do it.

Don't be shocked,
But I might be getting my tail docked.
So what's the big deal?
Will it give me more sex appeal?
Will it improve my mind
To have a shorter behind,
Or is it just a trendsetter
That supposedly makes me look better?

What d'ya say, bub?
Should I leave it alone
The way it was naturally grown
Or go for a furry stub?

Let's forget about rears
And talk about cropping ears.
Some would object
To ears that won't stand erect.
Does this at all affect
The way a canine hears?
Or is it done in certain cases
To aesthetically balance our faces?

I suppose
There are some pros
For this kind of lopping,
But goodness knows
Some oppose
And wish it would be stopping.

I honestly don't have a clue
As to what's the best thing to do.
Should I let my ears hang as they grew
Or surgically shape them anew?

♪ Remember,
I am the sunshine of your life. ♪

A farmer once told me
"Make hay while the sun shines."
On that point he sold me.
So ladies, just follow my signs.

Red Rover,
Red Rover,
let Rover roll over.

I hear that out west
There's a hound
That lives underground
On the prairie.
He enters his home
Through a mound
Where all of his bones
He must bury.
It can't be much fun
Living down there,
Hibernating like a bear.

See this bone
Here in my jaw?
Well, you'd better leave it alone.
When it comes to a feast,
Possession is at least
Ten points of the law.

I'm fit as a fiddle
Except for my middle.
It needs a whittle,
But if I work out
I have no doubt
That I can make it little.

Que sera, sera.
Whatever will be,
will be for me
since I'm as cute
As I can be.

Won't you please
Get rid of my fleas?
If you see a tick,
Remove it quick
Cause it can make me very sick.

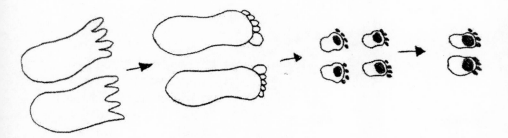

And the mutts shall inherit the earth
in spite of their canine birth.

The Three Tenors?

Harken. Harken,
I hear my neighbor's doggie barkin'.
Of course, it's naturally what we do,
And that's okay, but hey,
It's tough for those of us who
Must listen to it all the day
And all the nighttime too.

My mama done told me,
"No dogs on the beach!"
So she doesn't scold me,
This rule I won't breach.

Maybe one day
We'll find some shore
Where we can run and play
And people won't get sore.

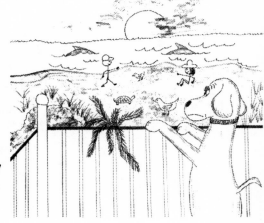

Oh, by gosh by golly,
Here comes the island trolley.
People are lucky to be able to ride 'em.
All we can do is walk along side 'em.

I'd like to run free,
But woe is me,
According to Ma and Pa,
A leash is the neighborhood law.

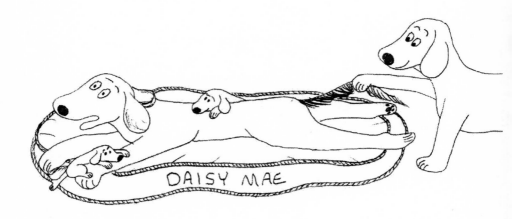

I'll have this job done in two shakes of a dam's tail.

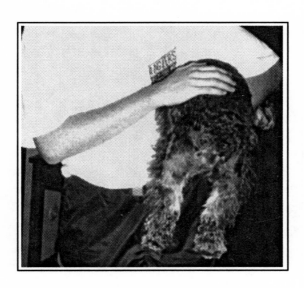

If hindsight is 20/20, then I must be a perfect vision.

It's turtle hatching season
And I'm a turtle fan,
So that's the reason
That every night
I dim the light
Just as much as I can.
I want my friends to be
Able to find their way to the sea.

Let's do *Paper, Scissors, Rock* to see who goes out for a walk.

Yummmmmm,
My lady's wearing her lotion.
For me,
It's like a magnetic potion.
I can't get enough
Of that intoxicating stuff,
But if I try licking it off
I'll be ticking her off.
So,
It's time to concoct a scheme
To get me some of that cream.

Peek-a-poo, I see you!

You scratch my fleas,
I'll scratch yours.
Just a little harder please,
I think they're in my pores.

Mmmm, a bonefish sounds delish!
I'd like it to be my own fish
served fresh daily on my own dish.

Beauty is in the eye of the beholder,
And puppies are as cute as it gets.
Our looks may change as we get older,
But we'll still be your loving, faithful pets.

If you want to see
Some very cute dogs,
Just look inside
The L.L. Bean catalogs.

I think today will be a bone jour!

I can take things with a grain of salt,
But by default,
I'll be using thyme
Because it works better with this rhyme.

It's a dog-eat-dog world out there.
I like mine with mustard and relish.

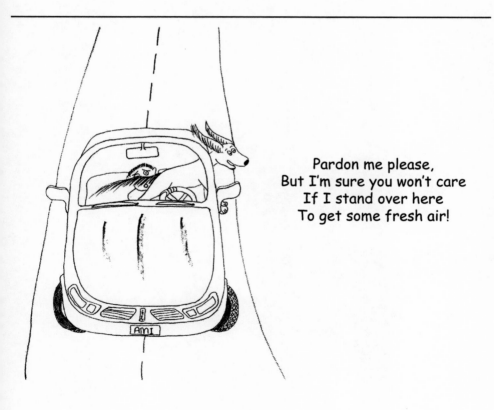

Pardon me please,
But I'm sure you won't care
If I stand over here
To get some fresh air!

Stereo types:
woofers and tweeters

Mum's the word!

So,
thanks for dropping by.

See ya next time.

TUGGER

Printed in the United States
66224LVS00002B/103-198

9 780977 852543